404 2083

For Hudson, whose story has just begun.
—T. T.

For my parents, who always picked me up softly.
—S. L.

union
square
kids

NEW YORK

Text © 2022 Todd Tarpley

Art © 2022 Sophie Leu

UNION SQUARE KIDS and the distinctive Union Square Kids logo are trademarks of Union Square & Co., LLC.

Union Square & Co., LLC, is a subsidiary of Sterling Publishing Co., Inc.

ISBN 978-1-4549-4418-8

Library of Congress Cataloging-in-Publication Data
Names: Tarpley, Todd, author. | Leu, Sophie, illustrator.
Title: Love is a story / by Todd Tarpley ; illustrated by Sophie Leu.
Description: New York : Union Square and Co., [2022] | Audience: Ages 3 and up. | Summary: Follows parents, grandparents, and a wide array of kids throughout all the seasons as they learn about the meaning of love.
Identifiers: LCCN 2022023709 | ISBN 9781454944188 (hardback) | ISBN 9781454944195 (board)
Subjects: CYAC: Love--Fiction. | BISAC: JUVENILE FICTION / Social Themes / Emotions & Feelings | JUVENILE FICTION / Family / General (see also headings under Social Themes) | LCGFT: Picture books.
Classification: LCC PZ7.T177 Lo 2022 | DDC [E]--dc23
LC record available at https://lccn.loc.gov/2022023709

For information about custom editions, special sales, and premium purchases, please contact specialsales@unionsquareandco.com

Manufactured in China

Lot #:

2 4 6 8 10 9 7 5 3 1

09/22

unionsquareandco.com

Design by Gina Bonanno

LOVE IS A STORY

by
Todd Tarpley

illustrated by
Sophie Leu

ü

union
square
kids

NEW YORK

Love is
the patter of ten little toes

as the first light of
day trickles in.

Love is the way that your smile starts to curve

when a giggle's about to begin.

Love is a puddle with you in the middle.

Love is a laugh in the rain.

Love is a track
with a big red caboose

pulled by a tank engine train.

Love is a morning that bursts into color.

Love is a dune

that we climb.

Love is a castle that's made from the sand
of an ocean that's older than time.

Love is a submarine under the water.

Love is a rocket to Mars.

Love is your hand
on a warm summer night

and a marshmallow
under the stars.

Love is a tree
with a welcoming branch.

Love is a
leap that you
make.

Love is a full moon that lights up the darkness.

Love is a treat you can take.

Love is a story
that's read with a flashlight.

Love is a warm teddy bear.

Love is a smile
and a sleepy-eyed whisper.

Love is a pillow to share.

Love is a shiver
that's warmed with a cuddle.

A mug full of cocoa just right.

Love is a sled on a cold winter day

and a quilt on a cold winter night.

Love is a hug
when you need it the most.

And the best part of love,
it is true . . .

If you give away all
the love in your heart

even more love will
come back to you.